The Relationship Syndrome

Tyrone Williams

Published by Tyrone Williams, 2023.

This is a work of fiction. Similarities to real people, places, or events are entirely coincidental.

THE RELATIONSHIP SYNDROME

First edition. December 1, 2023.

Copyright © 2023 Tyrone Williams.

ISBN: 979-8223054801

Written by Tyrone Williams.

Table of Contents

This book is dedicated to anyone who has ever been loved, hurt, and still made it out stronger than ever. Keep on keeping on. Always remember that beauty lies in the eyes of the beholder, for what lies beyond what you see is what you seek.

THE RELATIONSHIP SYNDROME

We destroy our own Hearts by perceiving thoughts rushed through the mainstream of overly saturated blood cells pumping through the veins. This love I had been broken by has left me standing in the cold rain wondering if I have the ability to ever love again. Feeling stranded and doubtful in whether my present life should remain the same. Though in the end we continue living life as a torn up photograph with a beautiful frame.

With so many heartbreaks before we have met, My passion for love is my only Regret.

And as I was left feeling benighted in the dark, a vision of past memories rushed to point out the blame...

THE LOVE
@reallygreatsite

THE LOVE

There I was standing in a crowded room watching her from afar,
Shone from a distance as though she were a star.
With all that she was so quintessential,
Like writing out my love story with a stencil.
The first sight of unknowingly doubtful love had my heart racing,
As she left the room I ran after her chasing.
And as I caught up I grabbed her arm and expressed myself like words
without spacing.
Similar views on life and love pushed our souls toward dating.
"It's you and me against the world no matter what the devil's creating, and
if all the ice in the world had melted we'd still be here skating".
These are the words I had spoken that day,
Even though we met in an unexpected way,
She was my sunshine on a cloudy day.
More beautiful than the sight of the solar eclipse,
My mind had lingered on the thought of her lips.
Smile so powerful it's heartbreaking,
When she left the room it left my heart aching.
I just can't get her off my mind,
Her soothing voice was one of a kind.
It's like nothing else mattered when I looked into her eyes,
Fell deeper in love it's no surprise.
A single kiss solidified everything we already knew we felt,
In a spontaneous moment I had lost all doubt,
As though I was ready to loosen the belt.

Yet I was the one who opted out.
Her smooth soft lips made me melt,
This is what true love is about.
And as the moonlight whispered slow soothing winds I stared deep into her
lonely soul as the stars aligned in the essence of romance.
Placed my hand on her face and kissed her with grace while a shiver down
the spine brought a joyful dance.
There was so much passion in this reaction with so much friction yet but a
fraction within this love my greatest endeavor became protraction.
I cared as much as I have loved warm heartedly,
Wherever life takes you, you'll always have part of me.
You deserved all the love I had given you,
I kept my promises and I had stayed true,
In love with the love that came from you,
As pure as a bowmore whiskey brew.
You loved me with no violation,
My heart had been settled in this relation.
You ran circles in my head on a daily basis,
You filled my heart with smiley faces,
You were the reason I forgot to tie my laces,
When I think of you my imagination takes me places.
I picture holding you tight each and every night,
Through every fight we always made things right,
You'll always be my sunshine and my moonlight;
You are my one true love you make my heart take flight.
To the height of the sky, the moon and the everlasting sun,
Until I die in my cocoon of love you'll be the one,
The one I gave all my heart, happiness and joy,
As I have left you like a boy leaves an old broken toy.
You were everything I wanted in this world filled with hate,
Let me just be blunt and say meeting you was fate
A well taught lesson I'm sure you can relate,

Yet it's never too late to start a clean slate.

THE LOSS

THE LOSS

All humans have different opinions of love. The definition of my love version is "bond". Money buys but bond is built to speak for your inner creek. As convivial moments were shared our hearts collided as the relationship came to its peak. With my history of being a soul searching dove yet bad at love I knew this bond would become antique.

In the same light I also discovered an important rule of attraction, communication is perceived by perception of tonality.

Vitality is the subject of a sudden change in this inquisitive reality,

She was as important to my worth as gravity to earth that's a sad irrationality.

On and on we went through all the technicalities,

Feeling vindication in upholding solidity in this relationship of abnormality.

The first time she cheated I stayed silent,

I asked a simple question and the response was violent.

Kept saying to me that I expect the worst,

As though this response had been rehearsed.

Her eyes, mouth and body showed it all,

My mind brought across a wakeup call.

Yet I remained here like a solid rock,

Built monumental strength like the birds flock.

Time moved slower while staring at the clock,

It made less sense than a round squared block.

Locked the brain on the feeling of letting go,

An experience we all know,

Seeking answers from the world,
To questions unfulfilled.
And to regain happiness,
To relieve the sadness,
We needed to part ways,
And find those better day we've been waiting for,
The love our hearts are aching for,
And the dreams that we're racing towards.
Monogamy is rare in this life we live,
It's so unfair you broke this life we built
All the struggles and trauma we've been through,
Now pushed to the corner like you always do.
That day I picked you up you had just come from him,
I could smell on your dress the perfume smell,
You acted as though nothing had happened but I saw through you,
My measure of emotional intelligence allowed me to sustain my hurt with
this smell now on my shirt as I sit here and question my worth.
I live my life by a commanding principle, "let go and let love."
How can I live by this when you're the only thing I love on this earth?
Continuous deceitful lies had broken the ties I never thought would be
broken.
For my remission of built up words will remain unspoken.
I am not a confrontational person.
I am not a stature of anger.
I am passive when situations worsen.
I am a delicate surface.
I remain I.
I will not change who I am for who you've become,
I am not done. I love on...

THE
HEARTBREAK

THE HEARTBREAK

A single soul can only hold limited introversion,
Which brings to question a blessing or lesson on this rainbow-pony
excursion. Endure hurt upon hurt,
Dragged through dirt yet still we give second chances.
Nothing as painful as viewing love through rose-colored glasses,
Imitation of having a love without recoil fades as time passes.
The love we lose is love we lost, by love we give, above whether the love we
receive is enough. (El armor se pierde por el amor dado)
And as ocean waves were splashing with a glow of the midst of the daily son
dazzling upon the waters,
Seagulls squawking as they soar above as regular boarders,
Distant psychologically blue mountains covering corners seen as round yet
has four quarters,
These insightive views brought internal thoughts being in this gasping
position,
Where past pains, present happiness and the unknown future came into
collision, alone in the sun with ink on paper to warm this cold division.
First fight, second fight, third fight, fourth.
Make-ups and break-ups made the heart switch off.
Like hanging on a cotton string this love was defined,
Winter days not as cold as a heart hard to find.
Four seasons came and four seasons left as the hate committed theft,
Stealing all the knowledge I had of love made darker by every breath.
A broken heart has taken away my pondering fear of death.
Like a lost soul soaring around in heaven,

My days on earth felt past due,
Felt like an act of transgression,
Someone save me from this depression.
If only I'd been given a warning sign,
That life is nothing like a straight line.
My biggest dream would be living in the stars,
Not chasing girls and expensive cars.
But then again we are who we are,
When life gets too hard we lower the bar,
Yet no matter how near or far,
We keep making wishes on that shining star.
And when the love comes back again it feels stronger than ever.
Late night phone calls talking for ages,
Making promises of staying together.
Like two lovers locked up in separate cages,
Distant love comes with stormy weather.
Like reading a book and turning the pages,
No love will last forever.
Conversations got dull and the interest became less,
Knowing that I was a second guess.
Unaware of what went wrong,
The distance between us too long.
Like Pluto from the sun it's inefficient,
This love had become nonexistent.
I still look at old pictures from time to time, I still feel hurt when I think
of you, and I still miss your smile. I miss your scent of aroma staying on my
clothes for later sensation. I still smile when I hear your name. I still wait for
your call or expect to run into you at the mall. Hallucinations had me stuck
in your lip balm hoping to kiss your lips just one more time. The love I still
have for you overpowers all the hurt you put me through. I still love you, I
do, I had hoped to one day marry you.
I always thought that I was destined for greatness,

Narrated by my own instructing voice,

This life I live like a romantic movie,

Slow country music playing as I settle for the next scene of feeling gloomy.

With my red headphones and guitar sitting in a bar having a glass of drought beer strumming and feeling droopy.

People would stare with sad eyes wondering "what has made this guy feel this way? "

I'd sit there squandering with no worry of what people would say,

Enjoy my cold beer and act like it's just another normal day.

As high as the sky my heart shall fly,

Never expected this love to die.

How can one person mould a hurt so bold?

A pretty face disguise with a heart so cold.

I gave all I could.

Never thought I would and there I stood looking stupid through bad and good.

My mind is messed up and my heart broken,

A well taught lesson had my mind stolen.

Thought meeting someone special was fate,

Until I realized we live in a world filled with hate.

Left discombobulated by the spiral of broken trust over the years as I have failed to create a key to your locked gate.

Kept telling myself it's never too late,

Met someone new and on the first date she had your favorite food,

And as I stared at the plate my mood became crude as my mind was glued to my undying infatuation.

It was only recently when I snapped out of that situation,

This feeling now feels like liberation.

And as my story goes on I'll go beyond my limitation with no expectation for the next chapter of our migration.

Yet some things always bring me back to you,

When doing the things we used to do.

Simple things like walking through the mall,
The way you'll stop at every stall.
Clipping my nails and leaving trails as a cute angry burst avails.
And as I gaze upon the moonlight,
All negativity fades away,
I see the light,
I rid the grey,
Happiness in sight,
Each night I pray,
That the one's left in my heart are there to stay.
Every day I ask myself this question,
Does true love really exist?
Or is it just an affection we can't resist.
Our hearts are often abused,
Because our minds get confused,
We deliver pain upon our lives when we get lost in the wrong eyes.
Real love means being a team,
Having a partner who supports your dream.
Thus lonely souls collide for a reason,
To build a love for an eternal season.
These are the words I had written,
Through the times you still left me smitten.
These words I will never forget,
I love you as much as the day we met.
I live my life with no regret and strum along with every fret.
Not a day goes by without you on my mind,
Never knew new love would be hard to find.
I fear that love will never find me again,
Grown weaker since the day you left me in the rain.
Some days something inside me just doesn't want to get up,
Another common feeling of letting go and giving up.
Maybe I am dead inside?

Maybe I should ready up for one last ride?
It's just too risky to let my walls down again,
I watched my heart slowly fall down the drain.
Without your love what reason is there for anything?
I go through life feeling like nothing,
Your appearance still heartbreaking,
I still want you to know I forgive you for everything...
If I go missing in my emotional state you'll find me at the waters,
Searching passivity in my missing puzzle pieces.
Just me and my thoughts in my lone discovered sanctum,
Yet still no tears as the hurt increases.
Boasting angrily into the air like a sky lantern,
And as time slowly decreases the heart rate your existence become a phantom.

STARTING OVER

STARTING OVER

Clouds turn into rain,
As my eyes burst out the pain,
From the hurt stuck in my brain.
These thoughts are like nails beaten deep into my undying heart.
Deeper and deeper as the train of thought makes a thousand stops in my head.
My eager heart turns to nothingness,
My mind dwells in this temporal anomaly unknown to how long or how fast or how strong or how vast.
Deserted from all emotion,
Brain dead forcing my body into motion,
Pointless to humanity like a peanut drowning in the ocean.
Like tree leaves shed in autumn my life had been renewed.
All idiosyncrasies dead to me as the flame of bond had died and cannot be resumed.
Sometimes you just have to let things go before the hate consumes you.
Sometimes you'll just never know when enough has happened to you.
Life goes on...
Most people see everlasting happiness as nothing but a fantasy,
Thinking that showing love and compassion is nothing but a hobby,
Well it's not ...love deserves effort, love deserves to be nourished.
No human in this earthly life can give you everything you've ever wanted or think you deserved, but this thought goes away when one puts in credible effort.

It all starts with a little bit, a little bit of passion to drive you to feeling a thousand butterflies in your tummy which leaves no room left for you to breathe as love takes your breath away. A little bit of emotion to drown the doubt of thinking that nothing lasts forever, and a little bit of shared happiness to cloud over the dark experiences in your future.

Additional Poems From My Private Notebook

Take a look into the heart of a poet...

PAIN OF MY SANITY

Pain of My Sanity

Rain?, pain!
Love leaves a stain.
All these thoughts of past mistakes rushing through the brain.
Let's flush it down the drain and stay sane as we search for a higher purpose on the life train.
There is no aim as perfect as the sky as we search wider than the lie and refrain from making the same mistake again.
Remain the main love of your life,
Don't seek a husband nor wife for love will find you on your darkest strife.
And as you stand baffled by the unexpected change you let down your walls and take off the chains,
Pain from the rain turns to joy on the train.
Cremate the past and leave the ashes in vain.

With Giving Comes
Losing...

With Giving Comes Losing

Love is lost by the love given,
By the flaws covered and scars hidden.
The hate we show shall flow like a river, or sow like a bird from the bad
words heard.
From a disguised friend we comprehend only after we send that hurtful
message, as we defend means of an end.
This could be it for us,
Since the moment I started to cuss.
Maybe this was all a rush; you're still stuck in your past this pain so vast I
just wish it could flush.
My heart beats like a unifying force,
For the love lost I'm steady in remorse.

Keep
Searching...

Keep Searching

We keep waiting for people to change,
Looking for motive to rearrange.
Always searching for someone to blame,
For your heartbreaks and downfalls it's a shame.
Some people live life like love is a game,
Some keep it burning like an endless flame.
We are all searching for that special person, the one who brings out your better version.
If only the signs were clear enough, I promise you won't shed another tear for love.
We keep searching for things impossible to find,
There's no such thing as one of a kind.
Were all similar in many ways,
Through smiling sunshine and sad rainy days.
Keep believing that miracles are possible,
And one day you'll overcome the impossible.

A Letter From
Love...

A Letter From Love

There is somebody special,
Out there waiting for you.
With an outside harder than metal,
And an inside bright sky blue.
Soft like a flowers petal,
If you promise to stay true.
This person keeps no secrets,
They will stick with you like glue,
So don't give them any reasons,
To disappear from your view...
With love,
Signed...love.

ONLY
IN MY
DREAMS

Only In My Dreams

There's no place in the world id rather be,
I'm happy in my dreams with the things I see.
All by myself I sit here in silence,
With thoughts that range from happiness to violence.
I've been seeing the world from a different view,
Where nobody notices the good deeds you do.
All that reflects are stressfull aggrevation,
Which leads to thoughts of a heavenly vacation.
This one thought bares a meaning so strong,
It keeps repeating in my head like an old love song.

Empty Cup...

Empty Cup

This life we live,
The love we think we deserve,
It's just a reflection,
Of your choice of direction.
We seek love in the wrong places,
Searching for beauty in the faces of different races.
Yet it comes from inside,
A feeling impossible to hide.
Always keep your head up,
Someday someone will fill your cup.

Tides
Of Love

Tides of Love

It's In the moment she looks into your eyes,
Which brings out the feelings you hide.
You remember heartbroken goodbyes,
How you learned to swallow your pride as you sit back and think of the lies,
And the passionate love which had died.
Don't live life in disguise,
Let go, explore and enjoy the ride.
Happiness may come as a surprise,
In the moment you're at your lowest tide.

LIFES

FLAWS...

Life's Flaws

Life has its ups and downs,
But we make it through the smiles and frowns.
Things always turn out to be okay,
In future times if not today.
My mind is always filled with clouds,
Always thinking at higher grounds.
Life is like an ongoing maze,
We keep searching for better days.

Left In Despair

Left in Despair

Left hopelessly with a bruised heart covered by a scar,
As I sit in the corner in an empty bar strumming on my acoustic guitar.
My love for you was like an everlasting flame, like a never-ending river, like
a sun that outshines all darkness.
Yet unforgotten love grows acres of darkness within me.
Here I sit thinking that love was to be benevolent,
When in the end my thoughts had been dispossessed by your envy.
In the end my thoughts had been compromised.
My heart had belonged to incompetence,
Unforgotten memories showers me in my sanctum of dessert sand.
Left alone in a broken glass,
Left to break in a broken car,
Left in despair by a broken past.

My Dog Star

My Dog Star

A soft love story if I may,
There I was going about my day,
It was a dark navy sky in the month of May.
Light showers of rain drops fell from above,
a dog star appeared and she caught my love.
I found myself in a labyrinth of emotion,
The first thought that came was the sound of the ocean,
Soft, still waters dissected my heart,
I could not turn to my known proclivity.
A smile and wave shared as our ways part,
As I depart to newly found passivity.
In that brief moment I had gone into space,
Vega, Arcturus and my Sirius A.
The brightest star on Earth yes I see your worth,
My benevolent love broke my lonely curse.
I had feared that love will never find me again,
But like Icarus to Earth a new star I have gained...

REM
DREAMS...

Rem Dreams

*Like a glass window building dust over the years then comes a little rain to
wash it all away.*
Some little figments of dust will still remain.
Such is true love.
It cannot be erased completely.
Love is a permanent stain.
I cannot live a life as though nothing is wrong if nothing feels right.
But neither can I call you sunshine if you won't be my moonlight.
I wake at two in the morning and stare at my tinted reflection glass,
Wondering how long this distant love will last.
Back into REM sleep to dream of another unreal draft.

Grimm Reaper...

Grimm Reaper

Death... I envy you.

As dark as an unlighted passage yet still you outshine life.

I resent you.

You get all the attention from another dimension my tears to suspension as my hatred overpowers my apprehension.

How do you do it in one day?

Years of tears held back by fears for cheers yet when you enter a room all joy disappears?

Still you receive the nicest words you lifeless turd!

People praise you more than life, they sing songs and give you joy from above.

Why is life not as loved?

One day I will meet you,

For I know that you are eminent and life cannot deplete you.

I'll look you dead in the eye as I discourteously greet you.

Although I walk through the valley of your shadow I pray my faith defeat you.

Alone In The Dark

Alone In The Dark

Confusion in the midst of another low night.
Blasted into space my thoughts I cannot face.
Drained and dried of all salt water.
Alone in the dark on a soul departed island.
Deep in the mind lies a thought of sole slaughter.
Alone in the dark on a soul departed island.
Who will be there?
Who will be there!?
Who will be there!!
When you're at your lowest point in life?
Who will be there when your fuel tank gets low?
Who will be there when your body no longer works the same?
Known thoughts to all man
Unfatherly questions to the boy who ran.
Wise is he who questions life
Cries could be the sharpest knife.
Alone in the dark on a soul departed island
Like a stone in a park my life gets stepped on
Like a bone to a dog my life gets chewed on.
Alone in the dark on a soul departed island.

The Patriot

The Patriot

We live in a world ruled by oppression,
Who unmasks other bigots by ostentatious selection?
Unknowing doing harmful damage to the lives of peevish patriots.
Thus we shall rise against these untenable actions,
We become chauvinists for giving a voice to our oblivion repatriates,
Be gazed upon in stigma for our indelicate reactions.
Embracing patriotism is a way to stand up for our nation,
Might seem insidious in its fastidious elucidation.
Standing up against supercilious beings,
In a scintillating manner expressing quintessential meanings.
We have endured racial epithets for way too long,
Let's keep singing the song, "together we are strong".

Bleeding
Heart

Bleeding Heart

Derogatory formations of words made me realise everything I ever wanted to say to anyone,
And anonymity gave me the courage to say it.
As I sit here empty and lonely caused by spreading the thoughts I had on my mind,
My heart so big and kind but love is still blind to me.
Why is it so hard to find enough to fill the hole of hurt I bleed from an undead heart?

See You In 20 Hours

See You In 20 Hours

A ten second hug feels like 50 years on Mars after a long day of work.
Let's put hugging down as one of your greatest quirks.
After helping you with dishes we'd spend a moment on the porch.
Looking up at the night sky as the stars shine down like an undying torch.
The hardest part of my day is saying goodbye to you.
I wish I never have to count down 20 hours before I see you again.
Goodnight my princess I'll text you when I'm home,
I left the spare key under the garden gnome.

Don't miss out!

Visit the website below and you can sign up to receive emails whenever Tyrone Williams publishes a new book. There's no charge and no obligation.

https://books2read.com/r/B-A-OYQBB-KGGRC

BOOKS2READ

Connecting independent readers to independent writers.

About the Author

Tyrone Williams is a 26 year old poet/author. He first began writing during his high school years and continued to extend his writing abilities privately. He has been through many ups and downs throughout his life but the pen and paper are his sanctum. After writing the first poem many more came in the darkness. He now has a mountain of poems that nobody has ever read and he is here to share some insight.This 26 year old man was born and raised in South Africa and continues to be a dreamer, dreaming that someone will admire the potential he holds deep within. Someone once did, and therefore he decided to make it official and call himself an author. There's an upcoming book release filled with action, comedy and romance. More news to come as the days go by.

www.ingramcontent.com/pod-product-compliance
Lightning Source LLC
Chambersburg PA
CBHW061405160726

47995CB00001B/471